HJØRDIS VARMER ~ LILIAN BRØGGER

Hans Christian Andersen

His Fairy Tale Life

translated by Tiina Nunnally

GROUNDWOOD BOOKS

HOUSE OF ANANSI PRESS

TORONTO BERKELEY

CONTENTS

CHAPTER ONE

In which we hear about stories and superstitions,

prisoners and lunatics —

and a poor boy from Odense

In the spring of 1805 a baby boy named Hans Christian Andersen was born in the kingdom of Denmark.

For the first few days after his birth his mother, Anne Marie Andersdatter, lay in bed while his father read aloud to her. Whenever the newborn child cried, his father would say, "Go to sleep now, or listen quietly."

But Hans Christian, like all children, would sleep only when he felt like sleeping, just as he cried whenever he felt like crying.

He also cried when he was baptized. The pastor did not take kindly to his wailing and said, "This child howls like a cat!"

The pastor's words angered Hans Christian's mother, for she loved her little son. She was a tall, thin woman, quite a bit older than his father, and she was very superstitious, as many people were in those days.

The boy's father, Hans Andersen, just laughed at superstitions. He was a quiet man who was fond of reading plays by the Danish writer Ludvig Holberg. He also liked to carve wooden toys for his little son.

When Hans Christian was old enough his father would take him to the woods on Sundays. He would tell him all about the plants and animals, while Hans Christian picked wild strawberries and threaded them onto a piece of straw. The boy also made wreaths of flowers, and little boats from reeds, which he would sail in the river behind their house.

Once a year his mother would go with them to the woods. She would wear her brown dress with the flower pattern, which was the only nice dress she

owned. She had that dress all the years that Hans Christian lived at home in Odense, wearing it only on her annual excursion to the woods or when she went to church to receive Communion.

On the way back from their forest outings Hans Christian's mother would gather branches from a beech tree. She would put them behind the shiny black stove at

home. Up in the ceiling rafters she hung a plant called orpine, or livelong, that she used to predict the future. She claimed that the herbs could tell her how long the people she knew would live.

Anne Marie Andersdatter had never known her own father, and her mother died in the Bogense poorhouse. When Hans Christian grew up and wrote his autobiography, *The Fairy Tale of My Life*, he didn't even mention this grandmother.

Hans Christian's other grandmother, Anne Cathrine Nommensdatter, lived nearby in Odense. She was very fond of her grandson and spent a great deal of time with him. It was her heart's desire that he become somebody grand, because she was vain and wished that she were more refined. She had a lively imagination and told the boy many stories that were far from the truth.

Hans Christian's grandfather was mentally ill all the years that his grandson knew him. He would take long, lonely walks in the woods, and when he returned home, he would often be wearing a wreath of flowers on his head. One time he walked through the town streets wearing a big conical hat made of paper. The street urchins jeered at him and ran after him. Hans Christian witnessed this scene, hiding in a doorway. He was afraid they would catch sight of him and start yelling at him, too.

Only once did Hans Christian ever speak of his grandfather. He was afraid of the eccentric old man, and he worried that one day people might call him mad, as well.

Hans Christian also had a half-sister who was his mother's daughter. The girl's name was Karen Marie. She never lived in the same house as Hans Christian. They did know each other, although he doesn't mention her in *The Fairy Tale of My Life*.

But he did write a good deal about his father and mother.

As a child, his father's greatest wish had been to go to grammar school, but his family couldn't afford to send him. That's why he became a shoemaker — a job that he hated. He spent all his free time reading and playing with his little son.

Hans Christian's mother could neither read nor write, and she thought it was foolish to spend time on such things.

But his parents agreed on one thing. They did everything they could to make their son's life as pleasant as possible, and they both spoiled him.

Anne Marie kept their small house clean and tidy. She washed and ironed the white curtains and decorated the house with knick-knacks and glassware and pretty cups. The house had only a kitchen and one other room, where they all ate and slept. And that room was also where Hans Andersen had his cobbler's workshop.

In the evening Hans Christian would fall asleep in his parents' bed. Later they would move him to his own bed on the bench against the wall, where his father sat and worked late into the night, even though he could hardly see in the faint light of the tallow candle.

From the kitchen a ladder led up to the attic. And in the eaves between their house and the neighbor's, his mother had placed a box filled with earth where she planted leeks and parsley.

Hans Christian's father read aloud to him on Sundays, and his mother often told him stories, including tales from her childhood.

Her family was so poor that she had once been sent out to beg. This was a dreadful memory. She could not bring

herself to ask strangers for money, and she ended up crying under a bridge. She sat there all day long.

Little Hans Christian had a lively imagination, just like his grandmother. He could easily picture how much his mother had suffered, and the story made him cry, too.

"But things are much better for you than they were for me," said his mother. Hans Christian, looking around their humble home, had to agree.

He didn't have to beg, and he had a father who drew pictures for him and carved toys out of wood. The pictures would move if you pulled on a string. There was also a toy windmill that could spin, and when it did, the miller would dance.

When Hans Christian was older he began to sew costumes for the puppets that his father made for him. His grandmother gave him scraps of cloth, which he used to make the finest clothes.

He also loved to spend time in the garden. He used a broom handle to hang his mother's apron in front of a gooseberry bush, making a cave where he would sit and dream for hours. He could see the buds sprouting in the springtime. He saw the berries ripen, and he saw the leaves turn yellow and fall off the bush when autumn came.

Hans Christian often sat with his eyes closed. Then he would envision things that didn't normally happen in Odense. Sometimes he even kept his eyes closed as he walked along the street. That way he could forget how poor his family was. He lived in the world of his imagination, where there was always plenty of food and everything was radiant and abundant.

But when he walked down the street with his eyes closed, the neighbors started to talk. "That boy must have bad eyes," they said. They couldn't understand what was the matter with Hans Christian. He wasn't like other children.

There was something else that made Hans Christian different. He was an only child, and that was unusual in those days. He was the center of his parents' lives and was given all the love they had to offer.

At that time Odense had a population of only five thousand, but even so it was the second-largest town in Denmark. Its narrow streets were paved with cobblestones and lined with small, crooked buildings. The gutters were filled with garbage, and there was constant noise from the horsedrawn wagons clattering down the lanes.

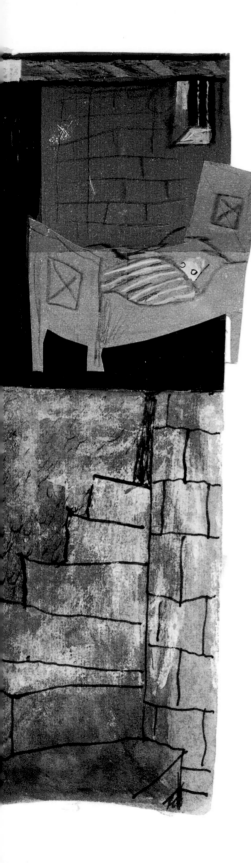

Hans Christian grew up in the poor section of town, and he never tired of admiring the great palace where the governor lived. People called the governor "the prince," and from his earliest childhood Hans Christian dreamed of being as rich and as grand as he was.

There was also a jail in Odense. The mere sight of it made Hans Christian shudder with fear as he imagined the prisoners inside.

One time the caretaker of the jail invited Hans Christian and his parents to a baptism. The boy was quite young, but he never forgot the evening. A storm had come up, and it was very dark when they arrived. The enormous, heavy gate creaked open, and the big key ring clanked as the door was locked behind them.

They walked up a steep staircase and sat down at a table, where two prisoners served the food. It was a lovely dinner, but Hans Christian, who usually had a good appetite, wasn't the least bit hungry.

A little later his mother put him to bed in the caretaker's bedroom. There he lay, imagining that he could hear the prisoners singing in the dark. It was both horrifying and thrilling, and he was completely exhausted by the time his father came to carry him home.

Hans Christian had more fun when his grandmother took him to town on feast days.

To celebrate Shrovetide, just before Lent, the

butchers would lead a fat ox through the streets of the town. The animal was adorned with birch twigs and flowers. Sitting astride the ox rode a little boy wearing a white shirt, with angel wings attached. This made Hans Christian's imagination sparkle.

Fishermen and sailors came to town for the occasion, and there were flags and music, noise and entertainment.

One Shrovetide a board was placed between two boats in the river. A couple of hardy men climbed on top and started fighting, until one of them was shoved off into the ice cold water.

At New Year the town's musicians would dress up in fancy clothes, with striped pants and yellow ribbons on their jackets. And on Easter morning Nun Hill was crowded with people who gathered to see the dancing sun.

Hans Christian loved these kinds of celebrations, but he didn't like being sent to town for buttermilk in the

evening. He had to go past Nun Hill, and people said that a ghostly light burned on top of it. He was so frightened he had to run the whole way until he had crossed the river. Then he felt calmer, because he knew that elves and spirits couldn't cross water. That's what his grandmother had told him.

She also told Hans Christian many other stories that made him shiver with dread and shout with joy. She had seen great splendor and wealth in her day — if her stories were to be believed, that is. And every Saturday she brought him flowers.

Hans Christian also went along to the hospital where his grandmother worked. It was where the crazy people lived. He would play in the hospital garden, and he enjoyed the beautiful flowers there, too.

Some of the patients would come out to see him. They told him stories and then they listened to his tales. Hans Christian loved to tell stories and sing for an audience. If he couldn't remember any of the stories that his father had told him, he would make up new ones.

The patients said that he was a clever child, and it pleased him to hear that. He also liked to hear them talk about superstitions and sorcery. But eventually he became so afraid of the dark and evil spirits that he didn't dare go out at night.

Twice a year the hospital was thoroughly cleaned and the trash was burned in the garden. This was an event that Hans Christian never missed. He helped make the bonfire, and was given good food to eat.

Sometimes he would go inside, with the guard, where the truly insane were kept locked up. There was a long corridor between the cells, and one day Hans Christian lay on his stomach and peered under one of the doors. Inside the little room a naked woman with long hair was sitting on a pile of straw, singing.

Suddenly she leaped up, and with a scream ran toward him. She opened the slot through which her food was served and stretched out her arms. To his horror the boy felt the woman's fingers grabbing at his clothes. He pressed himself flat against the floor and screamed in terror. When the guard returned, Hans Christian was practically dead of fright and had to be carried out of the building. That was an experience he never forgot.

Soon after, Hans Christian's mother decided it was time for him to go to school.

Inside the schoolhouse the schoolmistress sat in a high-backed chair. Behind her a heavy rod hung on the wall, but Hans Christian's mother had forbidden the schoolmistress to hit her son. There was a big clock and every hour when it would strike, little figures would appear and twirl around.

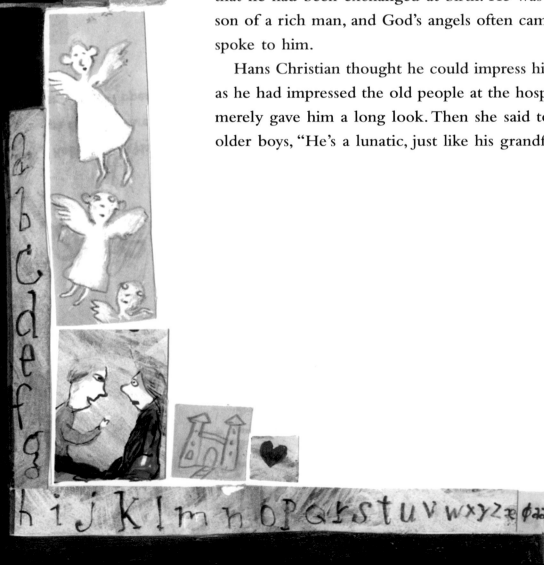

Most of the pupils in the school were girls. All the children were instructed to spell in unison, and if they didn't spell a word correctly, they were hit with the rod.

One day the schoolmistress forgot what Hans Christian's mother had said and struck him across his fingers. He got to his feet, gathered up his books and went home. The following day his parents sent him to a different school.

In the new school there were lots of boys and only one girl. Hans Christian was much younger than the boys, so he and the girl struck up a friendship. He drew pictures for her and told her stories. One day he drew a palace and said that he had been exchanged at birth. He was actually the son of a rich man, and God's angels often came down and spoke to him.

Hans Christian thought he could impress his friend, just as he had impressed the old people at the hospital. But she merely gave him a long look. Then she said to one of the older boys, "He's a lunatic, just like his grandfather."

CHAPTER TWO

In which we hear about a comet,
a wise woman, a peculiar child —
and a great sorrow

Even though Hans Christian seldom played with the other boys at school, he did occasionally tell them stories. But they laughed at his strange tales and his active imagination, and they would run after him, shouting, just as they ran after his grandfather.

In those days the poor people in town were allowed to glean grain from the fields during the harvest season. One day Hans Christian was out in a big field with his mother and other poor people. They walked along, collecting whatever the harvesters had left behind.

Suddenly the overseer appeared. He was a bad-tempered fellow who struck people with his riding whip whenever he had a chance.

Everyone fled in all directions. Hans Christian tried to run, too. But his wooden clogs kept falling off, because they were much too big.

The overseer raised his whip, ready to strike, when Hans Christian said, "How dare you strike me when God is watching!"

The angry man lowered his whip, patted the boy on the cheek and asked his name. Then he gave Hans Christian a few *skillings* and went on his way.

When Hans Christian told his mother what had happened, she said to the other women, "He's a peculiar child, my Hans Christian. Everyone is kind to him. Even that evil man gave him money!"

When Hans Christian was six, a great comet appeared in the skies over Denmark. The boy stood with his parents and their neighbors

in front of the cemetery and watched the blazing ball of light, with its long tail, race across the heavens.

His mother had told him that it might smash the earth into thousands of pieces — or that it could be an omen of terrible things to come. And as the comet shot across the sky, his mother and the neighbors said that the Day of Judgment would soon arrive.

But Hans Christian's father said it was all nonsense. He explained what a comet really was and said there was nothing to fear.

"There are plenty of things much more dangerous than comets," he said, walking away from the others. "Such as drinking and gambling. Those are truly evil things for poor folks."

The neighbors only shook their heads and went back to their conversations. They didn't understand what Hans Andersen was talking about.

Later that evening Hans Christian sat on his grandmother's lap and listened as she and his mother talked about the Judgment Day, which was now at hand. It was clear what they meant. This was something he could understand.

His mother also believed in fortune-tellers. One day a fortune-teller came begging at the home of the poor shoemaker's family. People said she was a witch, but Anne Marie gave her something all the same. In return, the woman agreed to tell Hans Christian's fortune.

"He will become a great man," she said. "And one day all of Odense will be lit up in his honor."

Hans Christian was pleased with this prediction. He

had already decided that someday he was going to be famous. His mother wept with joy, but his father said it was nothing but humbug.

Hans Christian was seven when his parents took him to the theater for the first time. He wore a new suit that an old seamstress had made from some of his father's clothes. His mother had fastened some scraps of silk to his chest to make a vest. Around his neck he wore a strip of black cloth tied in a huge bow, and he had scrubbed his face with soap and water and combed his hair.

The play they went to see was by Ludvig Holberg, Hans Andersen's favorite playwright. At first it was the crowd of people in the theater that made the biggest impression on Hans Christian. He looked at the audience and exclaimed, "If we had as many tubs of butter as there are people here tonight, I'd have plenty to eat!"

Hans Christian grew to love the theater, even though he was only allowed to see one play a year. But he became good friends with the man who distributed the handbills to advertise each evening's performance. Every day Hans Christian would deliver handbills in his neighborhood, and in return he was allowed to keep one. He would read the title of the evening's performance and then imagine what might happen in the play. At night he would sit at home and study his collection of handbills.

Hans Christian often had to stay home because he was ill. For several years he had suffered from strange fits. His mother never took him to a doctor, because that would cost money. Besides, she didn't believe in doctors. She had greater faith in conjurors and wise women.

And so Hans Christian was taken to see a woman who measured his arms and legs with a piece of string. Then she gave him a pouch containing earth from the cemetery and the heart of a mole. She told him to carry the pouch next to his heart, and that would undoubtedly cure him.

But it did no good. He still suffered from convulsions. His eyelids trembled, and he felt faint. This was during the winter, when times were hard in the family's humble home, and there was no money to seek further help.

In the evenings Hans Christian would sit and listen to his father tell stories. One time when the windows had frosted over, his father showed him how the ice crystals formed a pattern that looked like a maiden stretching out her arms.

"It looks like she's coming to get me," he said in jest, and Hans Christian and his mother both laughed.

Hans Christian's father admired Napoleon, the emperor of France, but he was worried about his invasion of Russia. With much of Europe at war, would he be able to support his family?

One day a rich landowner offered him a large sum of money if he would take his son's place in the Danish army. Hans Christian's father couldn't turn down such an offer, and in 1812 he became a soldier.

Around this time Anne Marie took her son to consult another wise woman.

"The only thing that will cure his nerves is water from the holy spring of Saint Regisse," she said.

So Hans Christian's mother took him to the spring on Midsummer's Eve. There was going to be a fair in the village nearby, and they could hear the sound of hammering and sawing as people set up their booths.

Hans Christian stood behind some shrubs while his mother undressed him. Then she led him to the cold, fresh spring water and ducked his head under.

But that was only half the cure. For the treatment to have a lasting effect, Hans Christian and his mother would have to sleep at the spring.

Anne Marie gathered some straw into a heap and then lay down on the makeshift bed with Hans Christian. Someone had lit a fire, and a coffee pot was bubbling merrily.

Hans Christian fell asleep, but during the night a terrible storm blew up, with thunder and lightning. A girl sleeping nearby suddenly began screaming wildly.

Hans Christian was so shocked that his whole body began to shake, and his night at the spring of Saint Regisse ended without a cure.

Eventually autumn arrived. Hans Andersen's regiment had been posted in Odense all year long, but now it was being sent to Holsten.

Hans Christian was eight years old and sick in bed with the measles when his father came to say goodbye. Fever made the boy delirious, and he had blisters on his lips. His father kissed him so hard that the boy's lips split open and started to bleed.

Hans Andersen rushed out of the house while Hans Christian lay in bed, listening to the drum rolls as the regiment marched away.

"He's out of his mind," said the neighbor women. "What is he thinking of, running off like that to get himself shot?"

But Hans Andersen did not get shot. He came back home several months later, although he was a changed man. The long marches had taken their toll on his strength, and he looked pale and gaunt.

He fell ill and lay in bed, raving with fever. He thought he was in charge of an army, and he kept shouting orders and issuing commands.

Anne Marie shook her head, thinking he had gone mad, just like his father.

Once again she sent Hans Christian to see the wise

woman. The woman tied a string around the boy's wrist and placed a green leaf on his chest saying, "This is from the Cross of Christ."

"Is my poor father going to die?" asked Hans Christian, sobbing.

At first the woman refused to say anything. Then she told him, "Walk home along the river. If your father is about to die, you will meet his apparition on the way."

Hans Christian ran off, terrified. He couldn't stop thinking about his father. His father knew that he was afraid of ghosts, and he would never have the heart to appear in the form of a phantom down by the river.

"Did you meet anyone on your way back?" asked his mother when the boy came home.

"No," replied Hans Christian. Then he begged her to send for a doctor, but Anne Marie wouldn't hear of it.

Three days later his father died. He was only thirty-four years old.

All night long Anne Marie sat by her husband's deathbed. When a cricket began chirping, she said, "He's dead. You don't have to sing for him anymore. The ice maiden has taken him."

At his father's funeral, Hans Christian practically

dissolved in tears. And when his father was taken to the cemetery to be buried, he walked behind the coffin wearing a hat, which his mother had wrapped in black fabric.

Back at home both Hans Christian and his mother wept and wailed. But his grandmother, who was deathly pale, didn't make a sound.

She planted roses on her son's grave. Later other people were buried in the same place, and eventually the whole cemetery became overgrown with grass and weeds.

CHAPTER THREE

In which we hear about a play,
and a puppet theater, a stepfather —
and a visit to the governor's palace

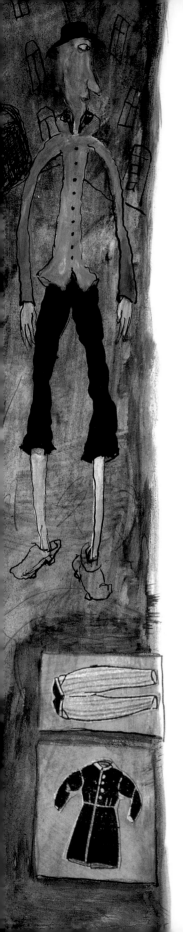

Hans Christian was now eleven years old. He was very tall for his age and thin and gangly. He had a big nose and long blond hair. He looked quite strange as he walked along the streets. His shirt was too small, and his wooden clogs were much too big. His pants were too short for his long legs, and he had an awkward gait.

In the mornings Hans Christian attended classes at the school for the poor children in town. But the rest of the day he was left to his own devices. His mother had to go out to do washing for other people, so Hans Christian stayed home, playing with the puppet theater that his father had made for him. He was so good at sewing costumes for the puppets that his mother told him he should become a tailor when he grew up. But that was not what he wanted to be.

He still had a vivid imagination and continued to tell his classmates the strangest tales. In his stories he was always the hero.

He had no friends his own age, but he actually preferred to be with grownups. And they were fond of the unusual boy who told them stories and sang for them.

Whenever one of the patients at the hospital had a birthday, Hans Christian would bring a flower wreath or a few berries threaded on a piece of straw.

And on his teacher's birthday, the boy would give him a poem. Sometimes the teacher, who wrote poetry himself, would laugh at the poem.

But Hans Christian thought it was almost an honor to be laughed at by a real poet.

He had become a good reader. He also had a talent for

reciting his lessons from memory, which made his mother very proud.

"That stupid boy next door is always slaving over his lessons," she would tell the neighbors. "My Hans Christian doesn't have to do that. In fact, he hardly has to study at all."

And that was true, although Hans Christian never did learn to spell properly.

He started visiting a widow who lived close by. Her name was Mrs. Bunkeflod, and she had been married to Pastor Bunkeflod, who wrote songs and poetry. Hans Christian had often heard his father talk about plays, but he had never heard him talk about verse. It was a pleasure to visit the home of a real poet.

Then he began to write his own plays. He read them aloud to Mrs. Bunkeflod, just as he read them to anyone else who would listen. If someone praised his writing, he would be giddy with joy, but if his work was received unkindly, he would weep with despair.

Once when a neighbor said something mean about a play he had written, he was beside himself.

"She only said that because her own son didn't write it," explained his mother.

That comforted Hans Christian a little. He wrote a new play at once, which he also read aloud to anyone who would pay attention. It never occurred to him that people might not want to listen to him.

Hans Christian was obsessed with the desire to read. He would go to the house of anyone who had a library and ask for permission to borrow their books. People liked this boy who wanted to spend his time reading instead of playing. When he looked at them with his blue eyes and eager expression, they couldn't resist his requests. One woman let him borrow every volume in her bookcase because he took such good care of her books.

Hans Christian sometimes wrote his plays in a mixture of Danish, German, English and French. He would look up foreign words in a dictionary and then use them to compose strange-sounding sentences.

One day he read a play in German to his mother. He put her apron around his shoulders like a cape, and when the hero was supposed to cross a river, Hans Christian stretched out on a stool and pretended to be swimming.

This behavior made his mother uneasy. She forbade him from indulging in such foolishness. No doubt she was thinking about his poor, mad grandfather.

One day she decided that Hans Christian should start working at a textile factory. That was where the neighbor's boy worked. She wanted to know what her son was doing all day.

Hans Christian's grandmother was very sad as she accompanied him to the factory. She didn't want him to work in such a place. At

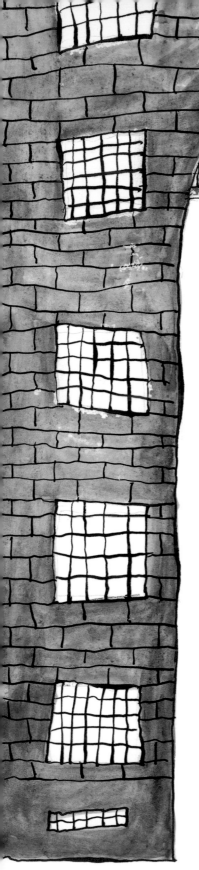

the factory gate she kissed him and wept, telling him that this never would have happened if his father were still alive. She knew that the boys who worked in the factory were a rough sort.

Hans Christian discovered that she was right. The boys told jokes that frightened him, because he didn't understand them. Then they would laugh at him.

One day, to appease them, he asked whether he could sing them a song, and they agreed. They had to do Hans Christian's work for him as he sang, but afterwards they all applauded.

That's how Hans Christian spent his first few days at the factory. But he also had to work, and the threads in the loom kept breaking. He couldn't figure out how to run the machine properly.

The others teased him.

"You have such a high, clear voice," they shouted. "You're probably not a boy at all. You must be a girl!"

And then they grabbed his arms and legs to find out if it were true.

Hans Christian yelled and screamed until they let him go. Then he rushed out of the factory and ran home. His mother promised him that he would never have to go back.

So Hans Christian continued visiting Mrs. Bunkeflod's home, where he read books and sewed costumes for his puppets. He also made a white pincushion out of silk, which he gave to the widow for her birthday.

A short time later Anne Marie found a position for her son at a small tobacco factory. There, too, he sang songs for the other workers in his beautiful voice and won great praise. He made up the words to his own melodies, and one day someone said that he ought to go on stage. Hans Christian thought this was a marvelous idea.

But then he fell ill again. His mother decided that the tobacco dust must be bad for his health, and so he stopped working at that factory, too.

When Hans Christian turned thirteen, his mother remarried. Her new husband was also a shoemaker, and once again he was much younger than she was.

Hans Christian felt even more lonely than before. He was used to having his mother all to himself, but now he had to share her with someone else.

His new stepfather was a kind person, but he didn't want any part in the boy's upbringing. Anne Marie waited on her

35

husband hand and foot, and Hans Christian felt left out. He played with his puppet theater or roamed through the streets. That displeased his mother, and she began talking about apprenticing him to a tailor, since he was so clever at sewing.

But Hans Christian had other plans for his future. He was still reading a great deal, and he especially liked reading about men who had grown up poor and then became rich and famous. He was convinced that his own life would turn out the same way.

Hans Christian's family had lived in the small house on Munkemølle Lane since 1807. It had a narrow strip of garden that led down to Odense River. That's where his mother set up her washboard. It was also where Hans Christian often stood and watched the big water mill on the opposite bank.

He loved to watch the wheel churning through the water, and he studied the fish in the river and the flowers on the shore. He often dreamed of elf maidens, and from here he had a clear view of Nun Hill, which had frightened him so terribly when he was little.

In the evening, when the weather was warm, he would stand on a rock down by the river and sing in a loud, beautiful voice. The neighbors called him a little nightingale.

Sometimes he was invited to sing in people's homes when they had guests. Even the town bishop sent for him. Among the bishop's guests was a young man by the name of Colonel Høegh-Guldberg. He was impressed by the fair-haired boy with the lively expression, and he invited Hans Christian to visit him. The colonel tried to teach him how to behave in more refined circles and to take an interest in Latin and geometry. But Hans Christian was more interested in princes and princesses and the theater.

One day Colonel Høegh-Guldberg told the boy that he had obtained permission for him to visit the prince, as the governor was called. He was to sing, and if the prince asked him what he wanted to be, he should say that his greatest wish was to study at the university. Maybe then the prince would offer to help him.

Hans Christian was dressed in his finest as he accompanied the colonel up the broad staircase to the beautiful palace. He sang for the prince, recited poetry and performed a few dramatic passages.

The prince asked him whether he was planning to go on stage. Hans Christian replied that he had been instructed to say that he wished to study at the university. But if he were to be honest, then he had to admit that his greatest desire was to go on stage.

The boy's remarks amused the prince, but even so he recommended that Hans Christian be apprenticed to a cabinetmaker. Then he could learn to make fine furniture. It was a good profession, and perhaps the prince could help him.

Hans Christian was deeply disappointed, although he managed to bow before leaving the prince's chambers. He had no desire whatsoever to become a cabinetmaker.

After all, he was destined to become rich and famous!

CHAPTER FOUR

In which Hans Christian travels to
Copenhagen, prays to God –
and almost goes mad with joy

It was time for Hans Christian to be confirmed. His mother gave him new boots for the big day, and a brown coat that had once belonged to his father was altered to fit him.

He was so proud of his boots that he tucked his pant legs inside to show them off, and he shivered with delight as he walked up the church aisle. The boots squeaked so loudly that everyone couldn't help noticing them.

Hans Christian was given a few more *skillings* for his piggy bank as confirmation presents, but the day was important for another reason. It meant that he would now have to find a job. He was too old to stay at home, idling the days away.

Life was hard for Anne Marie. Her new husband was a lazy man. She was the one who had to bring in the money to pay for the family's food and rent. She stood in the cold river all day long, scrubbing clothes for people in town.

But Hans Christian was the one who went to buy brandy for her when she was dead tired and shaking with cold. And he was the one who had to listen to the neighbors gossiping about how much his mother drank.

Hans Christian had only one desire — to go to the city of Copenhagen.

His mother still wanted him to learn to be a tailor, but he wasn't the least bit interested. His grandmother thought it would be grand if he became a clerk at the town hall.

But Hans Christian only wanted to go to Copenhagen.

He cracked open his piggy bank and counted up his money. He had thirteen *rigsdaler*, and he thought he was the richest boy in all of Odense.

Anne Marie sent for a fortune-teller. She read Hans Christian's fortune in the coffee grounds and said that his future looked promising.

So it was finally decided that Hans Christian would travel to Copenhagen. His grandmother hugged him tight and wept as he stood ready to leave, holding his little bundle of belongings. He was fourteen years old, and she had loved him with all her heart since the day he was born. Anne Marie accompanied her son to the edge

of town. There they said goodbye, and Hans Christian stepped inside the mail coach.

It was a beautiful day. The sun was shining, and Hans Christian quickly forgot the sad farewell with his family. At last he was heading for new adventures. The mail coach jolted along the dusty road. There were many passengers, and it was hot inside, where everyone sat crowded together on hard benches. It took a whole day to travel to the coast.

When Hans Christian boarded the ship that would take him away from the island of Fyn, he felt abandoned and alone. Now he had only God to look out for him. The ship sailed all night long, and Hans Christian was frightened by the sea.

When the ship dropped anchor at Korsør the following morning, everyone went ashore. Hans Christian slipped behind a shed in the harbor and fell to his knees, praying to God for help and protection. Then he climbed into the mail coach again. It took all day and most of the night to reach the outskirts of Copenhagen, even though they changed horses several times along the way.

On Monday, September 6, 1819, Hans Christian finally stood on Frederiksberg Hill and gazed out over the city of Copenhagen. He had reached his destination. Here he would make his fortune.

He said goodbye to Mrs. Hermansen, a passenger he had met on the journey. He had told her his whole life story, and she in turn had given him her address in the city.

Hans Christian walked through Copenhagen's western gate and left his bundle of belongings at an inn. Then he went into the city. There was a great commotion from all the carriages and people, but that was precisely what Hans Christian had expected to find.

He headed straight for the King's New Square and the Royal Theater. It was all he had been able to think about for so many weeks. He stood in the great square with the tall buildings all around and felt that a bright and happy future lay before him.

Hans Christian was determined to become an actor or a dancer. The very next day he went to see a famous dancer. She had no idea who he was. He wore a big hat that slipped down over his eyes, and on his feet were the

big, shiny yellow boots. He took them off and carefully placed them in a corner. Then he leaped back and forth and made wild gestures that were supposed to represent a dance. And then he began to recite poetry. The dancer thought he was mad and asked him to leave at once.

But Hans Christian was not discouraged. In Odense his friend, Mr. Iversen, had advised him to visit one of the managing directors of the Royal Theater. The man's name was Knud Lyne Rahbek, and he lived in a villa called Bakkehus in the suburb of Frederiksberg.

Hans Christian went to call on Mr. Rahbek. But the managing director wasn't the least bit interested in the gangly boy who stood before him, proclaiming his desire to go on stage.

So Hans Christian walked the long way back to the inn. He slept soundly that night, and the following morning he once again put on his confirmation clothes — the big hat and yellow boots. Back in Odense Colonel Høegh-Guldberg had advised him to call on the theater director, a man named Holstein, who was also a count. Hans Christian was certain that he would be received kindly.

He managed to get an invitation to the theater director's home, where he explained that his greatest wish was to become an actor. The count looked at the thin boy. "You're much too skinny to be an actor," he said.

But Hans Christian was not the sort to lose courage. "If you hire me and give me a good salary, I'll soon fatten up," he replied.

The count frowned, and Hans Christian had a sudden urge to rush out of the room. But this was his last chance to find employment in the theater, and he begged to be admitted to the ballet school.

"That's impossible," said Count Holstein. "The new pupils all begin in May, and they aren't given a salary until they've finished their training."

There was nothing for Hans Christian to do but leave.

A short time later he was once again in the King's New Square in front of the Royal Theater. What was he going to do now? He had almost no money left. Wasn't there anyone who would help him?

Then he remembered Mrs. Hermansen, the woman he had met on his journey. He would go to see her.

She advised him to take the first boat back to Odense.

"Never!" cried Hans Christian.

He left her house and went down to the harbor and stared into the black water of the canal. He would rather die than go back home and be ridiculed. He sat on the bank and wept. Surely God would help him, he thought. He had read that people often had to go through terrible trials before becoming famous. No doubt the same would happen to him.

He cried for a good long time. Then he walked back to the theater. He counted up his last coins and bought a ticket for one of the cheap seats, all the way up in the gallery.

It was a sad play, and Hans Christian got so caught up in the

performance that he sobbed loudly when things went badly for the young lovers on the stage. All the women sitting near him asked what was wrong. He explained that he had just arrived in Copenhagen, and how he could not find a job at the theater.

Everyone in the gallery listened to his story and then gave him fruit and sandwiches and cakes. This sparked new hope in him.

The next day Hans Christian once again went to see the famous dancer and Count Holstein. But nothing came of his efforts. When he had paid his bill at the inn he had only one *rigsdaler* left.

So he went back to see Mrs. Hermansen.

He had decided to learn a trade. It didn't matter what, because all trades were equally distasteful. But by the time he finished his apprenticeship, in six or seven years, he would be a good deal fatter. Then they would hire him at the theater.

Mrs. Hermansen received Hans Christian kindly. She even bought a newspaper so they could look for a position for him. They found an opening at a carpenter's shop on Borger Street.

The carpenter agreed to give Hans Christian room and board while he tried the job. But it turned out to be a brief apprenticeship. The other apprentices teased Hans Christian, and he felt as miserable as he had when he worked in the textile factory. He went to the carpenter and told him that the position was not for him.

Hans Christian had a new plan. He would become a deckhand on board a ship. He was sure that the ship would sink, so the good Lord would solve all his problems for him.

He prayed for help before he fell asleep that night. And then he suddenly thought of something. He had always been told that he had a beautiful singing voice. No one at the theater in Copenhagen had heard him sing yet.

Hans Christian had once read in a newspaper about an Italian choirmaster named Mr. Siboni. He gave voice lessons at the Royal Theater. Maybe he would help!

Hans Christian didn't want to return home without accomplishing anything. His mother would be sad, and his stepfather might jeer at him. And what about all the neighbors? They would surely laugh.

He had to find Mr. Siboni.

In those days there weren't many Italians living in Copenhagen, so Hans Christian quickly found out where he lived. Before he rang the bell, he knelt down on the steps and prayed.

The housekeeper opened the door. She said that Mr. Siboni had guests for dinner. But Hans Christian would not be dismissed so easily. He began to weep, telling the housekeeper everything that had happened to him. She listened and forgot all about her pots on the stove. Then she told him to wait.

She went into the parlor and told Mr. Siboni about the unhappy boy in the entryway.

The choirmaster and his guests went out to have

a look at him. They stared at Hans Christian and he stared back, shaking and crying.

Mr. Siboni took him into the parlor. The guests were all artists and composers and poets. The choirmaster sat down at the piano and began to play. He urged Hans Christian to sing, and then he listened without taking his eyes off the boy. After that Hans Christian recited several poems and a few scenes from one of Holberg's plays. Everyone in the room applauded. When Hans Christian heard their applause he started crying again.

All the strangers were kind to him, and Mr. Siboni said that he thought he could teach him to sing properly. He spoke in German, which was then translated. When Hans Christian heard what he had said, he laughed and cried at the same time. Mr. Siboni also said he was certain he could eventually find a place for the boy at the Royal Theater.

Among the guests that evening was the well-known

composer, Mr. Weyse, who was very friendly toward Hans Christian.

The housekeeper later told him that if he called on Mr. Weyse the following day, the composer would undoubtedly offer to help.

Early the next morning Hans Christian went to see Mr. Weyse. And the housekeeper was right! At the party the night before, he had arranged for a collection to be taken up among the guests. He had seventy *rigsdaler* for Hans Christian.

"Now you must find lodgings at a good place in town," said the composer. "Every month I'll give you ten *rigsdaler*. That way you'll be able to make ends meet."

Hans Christian was practically mad with joy as he walked down the front steps. He wrote a triumphant letter home, telling his mother how rich and happy he was.

He still had to find a place to live. Mrs. Hermansen didn't have room for him, but she knew of a place on the same street where he could find lodgings.

There were a couple of women of easy virtue living in the house. But Hans Christian was not particularly aware of them. He was so busy that he spent very little time in his room, which had

once been a pantry and had no windows and only enough room for a bed.

In the daytime Hans Christian took voice lessons from Mr. Siboni. He was also given instruction in German, and in his free time he helped the maids in the kitchen of the Siboni household.

That was how he spent his first winter in Copenhagen. It was a long, cold winter and Hans Christian's thin boots gave him little protection. His feet were constantly wet, and he caught cold again and again, which had an effect on his singing voice.

One day Mr. Siboni told Hans Christian that he would never be a professional singer. His voice was gone. And besides, he was too tall and gangly, and he lacked good breeding.

"It would take at least three or four years to teach you how an actor in the Royal Theater is supposed to behave, Andersen," said Mr. Siboni. "I can't keep you on at my expense all that time. You should go back to Odense and learn a trade," he concluded.

Hans Christian was crushed. There he stood, without money or education. What was he going to do? He couldn't write home and tell his mother that his good fortune had run out.

Then he remembered Colonel Høegh-Guldberg, who had been so kind to him in Odense. He knew that the colonel had a brother in Copenhagen. He was a professor and a poet.

Once again Hans Christian prayed to God for help. Then he wrote a letter to Professor Høegh-Guldberg.

Several days later he put on his confirmation clothes and went to visit the professor. The colonel had told his brother about this strange boy who wanted to be an actor, and the professor decided to help him. He took up a collection and then he arranged for Hans Christian to be given lessons in both Danish and Latin.

On his own the boy sought out a solo dancer at the theater. She fell for his charm and allowed him to take lessons at the ballet school. He must have been a peculiar sight. He didn't dare stand up straight, because both his vest and his pants were much too short. And to make matters worse, he went around wearing a huge fox collar that Mr. Siboni had given him. It kept slipping off and he was constantly shoving it back in place.

In his free time Hans Christian continued to make puppet costumes. Keeping himself busy distracted him from the fact that he was always hungry. But he remained optimistic.

"Things will get better soon," he would tell himself. And he would tell God how grateful he was before he lay down to sleep each night.

CHAPTER FIVE

In which Hans Christian is teased,
visits the princess —
and gets his name in the newspaper

Hans Christian worked hard as a pupil at the dance school, although he had little talent as a dancer.

But that didn't concern him. It was enough that he was allowed to go to the theater every day. He could watch all the performances without paying for a ticket, and he could go behind the scenes.

One evening he was even allowed to be an extra in a crowd of people on stage. He took great care to brush and mend his confirmation suit, and he also wore his big hat.

One of the actors shoved Hans Christian all the way up to the glare of the footlights and said with a scornful laugh, "Let me introduce you to the Danish public."

Hans Christian was so upset that he ran sobbing from the stage. He couldn't stand to be teased by anyone. He was terribly sensitive.

Yet it was precisely his sensitive nature that had made him so many friends. Most people were touched by him and charmed by his straightforward manner.

One of his friends knew a lady-in-waiting to Crown Princess Caroline and told her about the boy who could recite long passages of Holberg's plays from memory.

The lady-in-waiting was eager to meet him, and so he was invited to the royal palace. He immediately started telling his life story — which is what he always did — and then the Crown Princess came in to speak to him.

He sang and recited some poetry, and Crown Princess Caroline laughed and applauded. Hans Christian was not the least bit shy, and he left the palace carrying fruit and sweets. He had also been given ten *rigsdaler* in silver. He was giddy with happiness as he walked home.

But it wasn't long before he once again ran out of money. His friends advised him to petition King Frederik VI. But the king refused to offer him any support.

At the same time, Hans Christian learned from the ballet master that he would never be a dancer. So far he had been given only one small role in a performance, playing a troll, but it had made him happy to see his name on the handbill. One night he even took the handbill to bed with him, and in the flickering light of the candle read over and over: *A troll — Andersen*. But he would never become famous as a dancer.

Fortunately, his singing voice had begun to come back, and he was accepted on a trial basis at the Royal Theater's choral school.

Hans Christian moved to different lodgings again. The money he

possessed didn't go far, and what little he had he spent on books instead of buying food or clothes. He could almost do without food, but he couldn't do without books.

He was always cold and hungry. He often sat on a bench in the park at meal times so that his landlady would think he had gone out to eat.

Even though Hans Christian was now attending choral school, he was still determined to become an actor. He was given a chance to appear in several small comic roles, but they were not what he had in mind. He visited his friends, and they advised him to spend more time studying Latin.

"You need to know Latin if you want to study at the university," they told him. They all thought that he was very clever.

Professor Høegh-Guldberg was the one who gave Hans Christian lessons in Danish. The boy was now sixteen years old, and he was tired of endlessly copying out other people's work. Even though the

professor was a good poet, Hans Christian
found it boring to copy out his poems and
read through them week after week. He
asked for permission to compose his own
poem. It ended up being a tragic play,
written in verse. The professor was so
astonished at how good it was that he read
it aloud to his friends.

Hans Christian also read the poem aloud when he
went to visit Kamma and Knud Lyne Rahbek at their
home, Bakkehus. It had become a gathering place for
writers and artists. Hans Christian often joined his new
friends there, and they would always listen kindly to
what he had written.

Just as when he was a child, Hans Christian never
dreamed that people might not be interested in listening
to him read aloud. He was open with friends and
strangers alike. And he believed that everyone wished
him the best.

The success of his play in verse went to his head, and
he wanted to send the piece to the Royal Theater. But the
professor refused to allow him. Hans Christian thought he
was jealous that he hadn't written the poem himself.

By now Hans Christian had been attending the
choral school for some time, and he often appeared on
stage with the choir. For one performance he was dressed in a tight-
fitting leotard. Hans Christian loved to dress up in fancy clothes, and
he thought he looked splendid in this costume. He crept close to the
footlights so the king would have a good view of him from the royal
box.

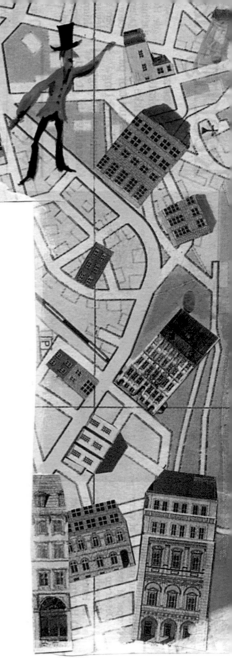

The king was horror-stricken at the sight of the bony young man sidling along the edge of the stage. But Hans Christian was undismayed, and he continued to call on Crown Princess Caroline and her lady-in-waiting.

He was also invited to many fashionable homes in the city. Yet when he was away from the footlights, he lived a wretched and meager existence.

Hans Christian was very proud of his many new distinguished friends. Before long he was spending so much time making social calls that he quietly stopped going to his Latin lessons. When Professor Høegh-Guldberg found out, he was disappointed and angry.

Even though Hans Christian pleaded and wept, the professor refused to give him any more help. He had believed in the young man and his talents, but now he felt betrayed.

Hans Christian sobbed, "If you forsake me, I will be left without a friend in the world."

But the professor would not be appeased.

"I will give you thirty *rigsdaler* more," he said. "But that's all."

Hans Christian prayed for forgiveness. Then he went to his Latin teacher and begged his forgiveness as well. He explained that it was difficult to attend to his lessons when there were so many wonderful plays at the theater.

The teacher consoled the boy, and from that day forward, Hans Christian set his mind on his lessons and studied the tedious Latin grammar. But Professor Høegh-Guldberg refused to see him again.

The winter of 1822 was particularly harsh. Hans Christian moved again, taking lodgings with a nice old woman. He often read aloud to her, and she would say, "You're a real poet!" And Hans Christian would weep with joy.

Otherwise there was little to be happy about. At the choral school he was teased about his strange appearance and eccentric ways. But he was still determined to become an actor.

On New Year's Eve Hans Christian sneaked onto the stage at the Royal Theater. Only a faint light was burning in the big hall, and he felt as if he were committing some sort of crime. But he had heard that whatever a person did on New Year's Eve was an indication of what would happen during the coming year.

He stood on the stage, unable to remember a single line. Then he

fell to his knees and murmured the Lord's Prayer. Afterwards he crept out just as quietly as he had come.

Surely his dream would now come true. Surely he would be offered a role. But he wasn't. And he had almost no money left.

He wrote a new play. One of the girls he knew made a clean copy for him, since his handwriting was nearly illegible, and he couldn't spell. He submitted the play to the Royal Theater, but six weeks later it was returned. The letter accompanying it said that it was not suited to the stage.

He was heartbroken. And he was even more heartbroken when, early in the spring, he was dismissed from the choir.

He had no money left. He wrote another play, which he sent to several people, including Professor Høegh-Guldberg. He was hoping that the professor would relent and forgive him. But the play was returned along with a letter that made Hans Christian weep inconsolably.

Then he suffered an even greater sorrow — his beloved grandmother died. He had never written a single letter to her, and now this tormented him. He couldn't afford to buy the appropriate black attire to mourn her death. This also caused him pain, because he always wanted to do what was proper. Now it was too late.

The summer was no better than the winter had been. Hans Christian never had enough to eat, and his clothes were so worn that they were practically falling off him. He washed and mended them to try to keep himself looking respectable, but it didn't do much good.

If only his play would be published and bring him a little money.

At long last he managed to have the first scene printed in a magazine. Seeing his name in print was a much greater event than seeing his name on a theater handbill. *Hans Christian Andersen — author!*

He was only seventeen years old, but his strength was gradually giving out. As a last resort, he decided to seek out Jonas Collin, who was one of the theater board members. He was also a powerful man in the government and personal adviser to the king.

Hans Christian called on Mr. Collin at his home, an old half-timbered house near the King's New Square. Mr. Collin was a somber man with calm eyes that missed little. He had read Hans Christian's play, *Alfsol*, which he now returned to the young man.

"This play would be impossible to stage," he said sternly.

Hans Christian thought all was lost.

"Yet there are several things that point to a certain talent," Mr. Collin continued, glancing at the trembling young man. "What you need is an education, and the board members of the Royal Theater have agreed to fund a scholarship for you to attend one of the better schools."

Hans Christian was completely bewildered, and for once he could find nothing to say.

Was he going to have the chance to attend grammar school — something his poor father had dreamed of doing his whole life? And was someone even going to pay his way and help him through the next few years? Would he no longer have to go to bed hungry?

He could barely contain his joy. Hans Christian rushed home and wrote a long, happy letter to his mother. He made it quite clear that his future was now secure forever.

CHAPTER SIX

In which we hear about the evil
headmaster Meisling, a visit to Odense, an execution —
and a return to Copenhagen

Jonas Collin was like a father to Hans Christian Andersen. At least that's how the young man thought of him. Finally he had found someone who truly had his welfare at heart.

Mr. Collin opened his home to Hans Christian, who quickly developed a strong attachment to Mrs. Collin and her five children. The Collin household was like none that hc had experienced before. Mrs. Collin was sickly, and so it was her husband who got up each morning and prepared tea and sandwiches for the children to take to school.

For the first time Hans Christian was in a home where it didn't matter that he was poor. The family liked him, and he was a welcome guest. To them, it didn't matter where he had grown up.

But there was not much time to enjoy his stay with the Collins, because he was going off to attend grammar school in Slagelse.

On the evening of October 26, 1822, the mail coach came to a halt in front of an inn in Slagelse. The journey from Copenhagen had been long and exhausting, but Hans Christian was in good spirits. His new life was about to begin.

The headmaster at the school was a man named Meisling. He was short and stout, with red hair and a round face. He had a thick neck and short arms, and he always seemed to be sneering. Hans Christian also noticed that the headmaster's hands were filthy. Only the very tips of his fingers were clean. This was because he was always squeezing lemon into his punch, which he drank every evening.

Hans Christian was given stacks of books on subjects such as Greek, Latin, history, geometry, French and German. It was enough to make him dizzy, and it took all the concentration he could muster to spell his way through his lessons.

He was placed in a class with the youngest boys, and that was a great embarrassment. Mr. Meisling also made a point of deriding

him in front of his classmates day after day, hour after hour.

This made Hans Christian study his lessons harder, but he grew more and more nervous. When the headmaster pelted him with questions his answers were barely intelligible.

He had promised Mr. Collin not to write poetry as long as he was attending grammar school, but he could not keep his promise. In the evening, after finishing his lessons, Hans Christian would take out his pen. He felt peaceful whenever he sat down to write a poem.

At Christmas he went to visit the Collin family. He brought his grade report along, and Mr. Collin was very satisfied. Hans Christian had been given excellent marks for his hard work and behavior, in spite of the fact that Headmaster Meisling did little but mock him in class. Mr. Collin loaned Hans Christian enough money for some new clothes and invited him to dinner.

Hans Christian enjoyed his holiday, which he spent visiting friends and attending the theater. But he soon had to return to the daily torments of school in Slagelse.

When Easter came Hans Christian made his first visit back to Odense. Princess Caroline had given him a little money, but it wasn't enough for the mail coach. He had to walk most of the way, carrying his small bundle of clothes.

At first his mother didn't recognize him, but then she showered him with kisses and tears. She could hardly believe that this fine-looking gentleman was her son.

She took him around to show him off to all her

neighbors and acquaintances, and Hans Christian willingly went along to be admired. People leaned out of their windows just to catch a glimpse of him. They all knew that his studies were being paid for by a scholarship from the king, and that was quite extraordinary.

Hans Christian's mother was in need of some good news. She was now a widow for the second time, and her mother-in-law had also died. Her poor lunatic father-in-law had been locked up in an institution, and her own mother was now living in the poorhouse. It was not a pleasant place to be. The inmates never had enough to eat, and the place was crawling with lice and vermin.

During his visit Hans Christian went to the paupers' cemetery to see his father's grave, but it was no longer visible.

He was received in the most distinguished households in Odense, and he enjoyed his holiday and the rich life. But when the Easter season came to an end, he was once again faced with long months of studying and the daily scorn at Headmaster Meisling's school.

Finally the summer holidays arrived, and in the fall Hans Christian was promoted to the third level, which at the time was the second-highest class. In his grade report the headmaster remarked on Hans Christian's great diligence. This made him happy once again.

Years passed. At the best of times Hans Christian floated on a cloud of joy and praise — but in the dark

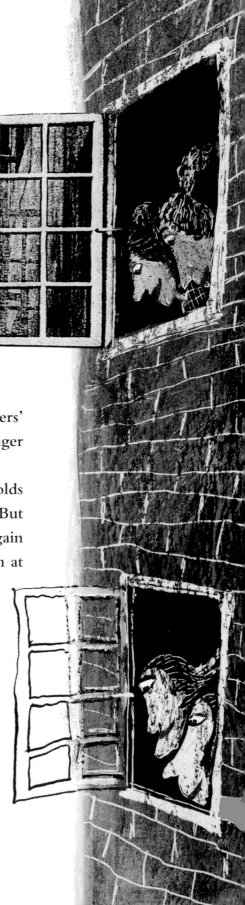

times, which occurred frequently, he felt as if he would never make anything of himself. And Headmaster Meisling did nothing to help him see things in a brighter light.

During his stay in Slagelse Hans Christian experienced an event that made a deep impression on him. Headmaster Meisling decided that it would be beneficial for his pupils to witness a public execution. There was going to be a triple execution in Skælskør. A seventeen-year-old girl, her sweetheart and a servant were all to be decapitated. The girl and her sweetheart had ordered the servant to murder the girl's father, because he didn't approve of their love.

Hans Christian and his classmates arrived at the town gates just as the condemned rode past, seated on the bed of a horsedrawn wagon. The girl was deathly pale, and her sweetheart was holding her in his arms. Behind them sat the servant. His skin was gray, and his long hair hung down over his forehead. Every time someone shouted farewell to him, the servant took off his hat and nodded.

Three pastors accompanied the condemned, as they each found their place beside a coffin and began to sing a hymn. The girl sang louder than the others.

Hans Christian felt faint. The girl kissed her sweetheart and the servant and the pastors. Then she lay her head on the block. The first blow of the ax fell!

Each of the young men, in turn, placed his head on the bloody block. The blows fell, and at the same time the crowd started pushing Hans Christian closer.

A poor sick man was given some of the blood to drink. According to superstition, human blood could cure many illnesses. At one time Hans Christian's mother had even talked about how it might help him but nothing came of it.

Then the young girl's grandmother placed her body in one of the coffins. The heads of the young men were set on poles, in disgrace. And the executioner and his henchmen dined on roast eel and brandy after a job well done.

Hans Christian slept very little that night. The wind blew hard and the tree branches banged against the windowpanes. All night long he saw the young girl's pale face and staring eyes before him. It was an event from which he never fully recovered.

Hans Christian faithfully sent his grade reports to Jonas Collin, who encouraged the boy to continue his hard work.

In 1825 Mr. Meisling was appointed headmaster of the grammar school in Helsingør. He and his family moved there, and Hans Christian, who was then twenty years old, went with them. He was to share lodgings with them, because they had discovered that he was good at taking

care of the children. And the family could also put to good use the two hundred *rigsdaler* that Mr. Collin paid each year for Hans Christian's room and board.

This was a difficult time for Hans Christian. He could hardly stand living in the headmaster's filthy home and being forbidden to write poetry. He tried to keep his promise to Mr. Collin, but it was not easy, and he ended up writing many poems during his grammar school years.

One of the poems, "The Dying Child," was translated and printed in a German newspaper, although the author's name was not mentioned. Hans Christian didn't dare show it to his friends in Copenhagen, since he wasn't supposed to be writing poetry.

Nevertheless, the poem did appear in Danish. It was published in the *Copenhagen Post* on September 25, 1827. Since that date, the poem has appeared in countless languages all over the world.

Eventually life at the school in Helsingør became too much for Hans Christian. Mr. Meisling continued to persecute him, even jeering at his need to write poetry.

"You think you're a poet, my dear Mr. Andersen," the headmaster said. "But you're not, and you never will be."

This made Hans Christian feel terrible. But he still kept telling everyone he knew that someday he would be a great man.

He wrote scores of letters during these years. He was particularly close to the daughter of one of his friends. Her name was Henriette Wulff, but Hans Christian always called her Jette. Her body was hunchbacked, yet she was self-assured and clever and had a good sense of humor.

When Hans Christian had to take care of Headmaster Meisling's children, he would set up the puppet theater that his father had made for him long ago. He knew many plays by heart, and he acted out all the parts himself. The children found him enormously entertaining.

One day a new teacher was hired at the school, and he noticed how badly Hans Christian was treated. He heard Mr. Meisling's daily remark that "Andersen is so stupid he has no hope of graduating." Yet Hans Christian did very well in most subjects.

When the new teacher was invited to dinner with the Meisling family, he saw that Hans Christian was begrudged the very food he ate and the wood he needed to burn in his stove. And he heard the way the headmaster ridiculed the young man in front of the maids.

The new teacher thought this was disgraceful, and he said as much to Jonas Collin.

Hans Christian had often complained in his letters to Mr. Collin. But he had never mentioned that he was living in filthy conditions, or that he lacked basic necessities. He had always written that he didn't consider himself worthy of the money that was spent on him.

Finally Mr. Collin understood that Hans Christian had endured much more than he knew. He immediately made arrangements for him to finish his schooling in Copenhagen.

When it was time to leave, Hans Christian went to say farewell to Headmaster Meisling, even though the man had treated him so badly. "I just wanted to say goodbye," he stammered, "and thank you for all you've done for me."

The headmaster leaped to his feet. "Damn you to hell!" he bellowed.

Hans Christian no longer felt ungrateful for leaving before completing his school year. He headed back to Copenhagen. A new phase was about to begin.

CHAPTER SEVEN

In which we hear about *A Walking Tour,*
a theater success —
and Riborg Voigt

Hans Christian Andersen was now twenty-three years old and lived in a rented room on Vingård Lane in Copenhagen. He studied hard and passed his final exams the year after his return to the capital.

His clothes were now nicer than they'd ever been and were no longer so glaringly different from what the other students wore. His health had also improved, since he finally had regular meals. In those days it was customary for the wealthy families of Copenhagen to help young students by feeding them.

Hans Christian took his meals with a number of different families, and in every home he was received kindly. People liked his open and honest nature. He never dreamed of hiding his innermost thoughts from his friends. And he was vivacious and talkative.

There were two families, in particular, that he enjoyed visiting. One was Jette Wulff's family, and the other was the Collin family.

Jette had been his good friend for many years. He

called her his sister, and they confided in each other. She
believed in him, encouraged him and wasn't afraid to tease
him a little as well. Hans Christian was deeply grateful to
her.

"You were the one who made me forget that I was a
poor and wretched stranger," he once told her.

The Collin family treated him as one of their own. He
became close friends with Edvard, the son of Jonas and
Henriette Collin. Edvard looked after him like a brother.
Everyone in the Collin family was fond of playing games
and teasing. At first Hans Christian was afraid of making a
fool of himself, but he soon discovered that the teasing was
all done with affection.

Even though Hans Christian passed his exams with
good marks, he still felt inferior, especially with regard to
Edvard Collin, who always did everything the proper way.
Edvard had helped him with his Latin lessons, and he was
particularly good at spelling and Danish grammar, which
made Hans Christian envious.

He still loved to perform. He never failed to have a poem or two in his pocket, which he would gladly read aloud. He showed his audience the greatest respect and always bowed solemnly when they applauded. Many people were amused by this awkward young man who was so willing to display his talents. But he never noticed their amusement. He heard only their words of praise.

The Danish writer Johan Ludvig Heiberg was the publisher of *Copenhagen's Flying Post,* and he accepted two of Hans Christian's poems. On the day they appeared in print, Hans Christian was having dinner with the Wulff family. Commander Wulff came into the parlor with the newspaper in his hand.

"Today there's something especially good in the paper," he said. Then he read both poems aloud, very enthusiastically. But the paper didn't mention who the author was.

"Andersen wrote them!" said Jette, because he had told her all about them.

The commander turned on his heel and left the parlor without a word. He was one of the people who maintained that Hans Christian ought to focus on his studies and not waste time on verse and other foolishness.

Whenever anyone acted like this, Hans Christian was deeply distressed. He couldn't understand why people wouldn't want to share his joy, and he would be dejected for days afterwards.

Hans Christian always had interesting experiences on his walks through the streets of Copenhagen, and he would

write down what he encountered or observed. His accounts eventually became a book called *A Walking Tour from Holmen's Canal to the Eastern Point of Amager*. It was published in 1829, when he was twenty-four years old, and it was a big success.

To express his joy Hans Christian wrote an operetta and sent it to the Royal Theater. The operetta was accepted.

On opening night, in April 1829, he sat in the wings thinking about the New Year's Eve when he had fallen to his knees on the empty stage. Every seat in the house was taken. Many of the audience members were fellow students who had come to pay tribute to him. The last lines of the play were followed by thunderous applause.

"Long live Andersen!" the audience shouted.

After this triumphant reception, Hans Christian rushed across the street to the Collin house. Old Mrs. Collin, who was deaf, had not attended the performance. She gazed with horror as he sank into a chair and burst into tears.

"Plenty of other authors have been booed off the stage," she said, trying to console him.

"But nobody was booing," he exclaimed, sitting up straight. "They all clapped and shouted, 'Long live Andersen!'"

Hans Christian began studying at the university and passed his first exams with excellent marks. But he didn't want to continue his studies. Even Jonas Collin, who had always insisted that he should train for some "respectable profession," finally gave in.

"In God's name, you must take the path that is destined for you," he said.

Hans Christian was happy to hear these words from his dear friend. And just before Christmas of that year, his first volume of poetry was published.

In the summer he went to Odense to visit his mother, who was now elderly. She clung to him and wept with joy, and Hans Christian lovingly responded by going with her to visit old acquaintances.

His mother was quite feeble. One eye was clouded with cataracts, which she tried to conceal with a big stray curl that hung down over her face. During his visit Hans Christian devoted all his time to her and gave her money, trying to make her life a little easier. And he pretended not to notice that she was drinking more than ever.

Hans Christian had moved to Store Kongens Street where he had two nice, bright rooms that made him proud.

After his last visit to Odense he longed to do more traveling. This time he wanted to see both Jutland and Fyn. He had plans to write a historical novel, and he wanted to see the actual places where his story would unfold.

78

He set off carrying letters of introduction to several distinguished families, and in Jutland he was graciously received. People knew his name and had read his books. He stayed with people in town and on great estates, enjoying living among the wealthy.

Following his journey to Jutland, he went back to Odense. He stayed with several of his old friends, including Iversen's widow and her two daughters. The young women laughed and joked with him, and he wondered if he might fall in love with one of them. But they simply enjoyed each other's company.

Hans Christian longed for love. He wrote in his diary, "Give me a bride. My blood and my heart yearn for love."

After his visit to Odense he continued on to the town of Fåborg, where he had a friend named Christian Voigt.

When Hans Christian arrived at his friend's house the only one home was Christian Voigt's sister Riborg. She was a lovely young woman who was twenty years old.

Hans Christian sat and looked at her as she poured tea for him. She had warm brown eyes and was wearing a beautiful dress and a little lace bonnet.

Riborg had read his books. She had great admiration for both *A Walking Tour* and his poetry, and she blushed whenever he spoke to her.

Hans Christian thought she was exquisite, and during the three days that he spent in Fåborg he grew more and more fond of her.

They took walks together and went rowing. Riborg made a wreath from oak leaves and asked her brother to give it to him.

After this Hans Christian practically floated back to the inn where he was staying. The maid was still awake when he came in, so he asked her if she knew whether Miss Voigt was engaged.

"Riborg's not properly engaged, although she has been seeing a lot of the apothecary's son," said the maid. "But he's not good enough for her. I think she's doing it to spite her father, who doesn't care for the young man."

Hans Christian couldn't stand to stay in Fåborg when he knew that Riborg was practically engaged to someone else. And so he returned to Odense and once again took lodgings with the Widow Iversen.

Her two daughters soon discovered the change that had come over their friend. They laughed and teased him.

"Andersen is in love!"

He replied with a jest, but deep inside he was astonished. Was he truly in love?

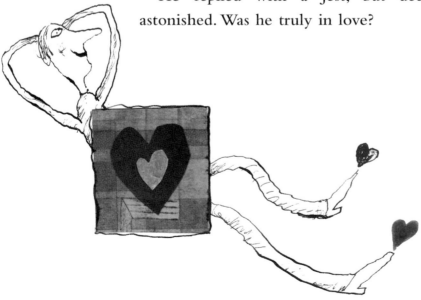

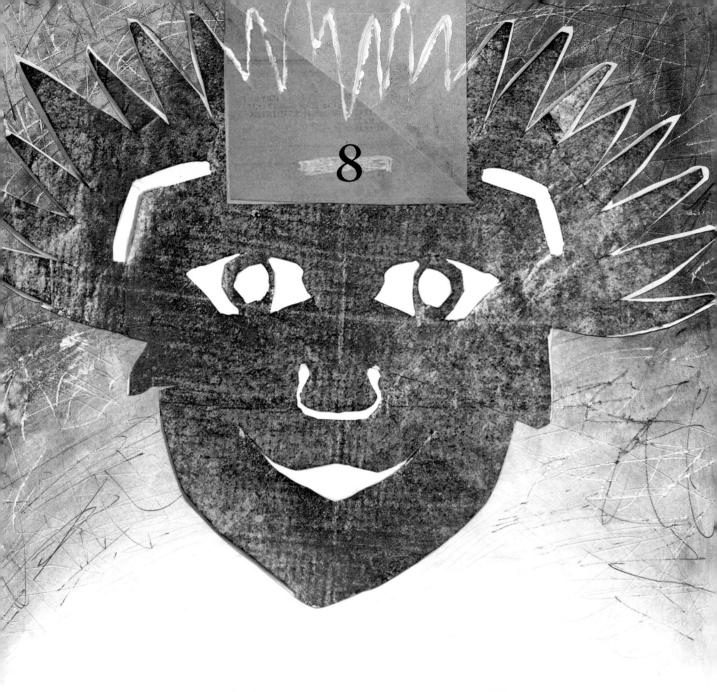

8

CHAPTER EIGHT

In which we hear about a great love, long journeys – and loneliness

Both Christian Voigt and Hans Christian Andersen spent the autumn in Copenhagen. They saw each other often, and one day Christian told his friend that Riborg had come to visit. She had said that what she most looked forward to was seeing Hans Christian again.

Hans Christian hurried over to his friend's lodgings. There sat Riborg with her sewing. She blushed every time he looked at her.

Hans Christian read aloud to her, and felt that he loved her more than anyone on earth. He vowed that he would even look for permanent employment if only he might win her hand. He would do anything for her. And he prayed to God for help.

He wrote a poem for Riborg that was a great declaration of love:

Dream of my dreams are you alone,
You are my heart's first love!
Like no one on earth, I love only you,
More than time and eternity above.

But Riborg was as good as engaged to the apothecary's son.

Hans Christian wrote a letter to her in which he expressed his hopes and his love. He wrote that he would be terribly unhappy if she refused to marry him. But he seemed to know that it wasn't meant to be. He ended his letter, "If only we might both be happy. You must forget this person, who will never, ever forget you... Live well!"

Riborg wept when she read his letter, but she couldn't bring herself to break with her childhood sweetheart. When she said farewell to Hans Christian, she clasped his hands in hers and gave him a note.

"Live well, live well!" her note said. "I hope that Christian will soon tell me that you are calm and happy, as you were before. With heartfelt friendship, Riborg."

They saw each other twice more, but there were always family members present, so there was no opportunity to talk in private. In those days it wasn't proper for a young man to invite a young woman out unchaperoned, unless he was engaged to her.

Riborg returned home to Fåborg and was formally engaged to her sweetheart, while Hans Christian wrote poems full of sorrow and despair.

He had another love besides Riborg Voigt — poetry. His love for poetry was possibly greater than for anything else.

If he had become engaged to Riborg, he would have had to find a job so he could earn money to support a wife and children. Instead, he was still free as a bird, and he made use of his unhappiness in his art.

But he never forgot Riborg. After his death, a little leather pouch was found at his breast. Inside was the note that Riborg had written to him when they parted. In accordance with his last wishes, Edvard Collin burned the letter without reading it.

That winter Hans Christian was in anguish. He had published a new volume of poetry, but it was received harshly, and he was mocked in the newspapers. The critics said that he was insufferable and vain. It was almost as if they regretted giving his first books such high praise.

Yet in spite of these hardships, Hans Christian was determined to reach his goal. He was going to become a great writer — and some day he would be famous all over the world.

Jonas Collin saw that the failed love affair and the harsh

criticism had taken their toll on him. He suggested that the young man go abroad.

Hans Christian thought this was a splendid idea. He had saved up some money, so he decided to travel to Germany.

In May 1831 he sailed from Copenhagen to Travemünde and then traveled by coach to Lübeck and Hamburg, across the German heath. The sandy roads had deep wheel ruts that made the heavy coach jolt from side to side. Progress was slow even though the coach traveled both day and night. The passengers could taste grit between their teeth, and when they finally reached their destination, their suitcases and hatboxes were brown with dust.

Hans Christian went to see all the sights, but he spent even more time observing the people he met along the way. His imagination was sparked by encountering so many strangers. He also visited several German writers and became friends with them.

The journey lasted only six weeks, but it made a deep impression on him. It was the first of many trips abroad. And it was the beginning of his career as a travel writer.

As soon as he returned to Copenhagen, Hans Christian published a book describing his experience, *Shadow Pictures of a Journey to the*

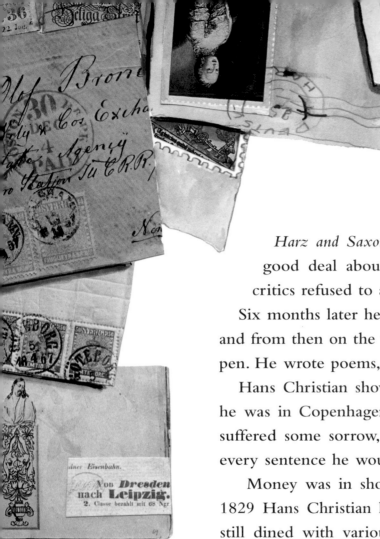

Harz and Saxon Switzerland. Although he talked a good deal about what a great writer he was, the critics refused to agree. Yet he continued to write.

Six months later he published a new volume of poetry, and from then on the words flowed continuously from his pen. He wrote poems, novels and plays.

Hans Christian showered his friends with letters when he was in Copenhagen and when he was traveling. If he suffered some sorrow, he didn't hide it from them. With every sentence he would reveal how unhappy he was.

Money was in short supply during these years. Since 1829 Hans Christian had supported himself, although he still dined with various families. For lunch he often ate only a little bread and sausage.

It was expensive to keep his rooms and clothing neat and tidy, and Hans Christian was very meticulous. Perhaps this stemmed from his memories of the tiny room with the starched curtains in his childhood home in Odense. He couldn't boast of coming from a good family, but he could still maintain a neat and proper appearance.

He was still friends with Edvard Collin, although they were as different as night and day. Once Hans Christian suggested that they address each other informally, but Edvard refused. It was important to him to keep a slight distance from Hans Christian, who could often be a difficult friend. Whenever he faced a setback, he would complain. Edvard couldn't bear to listen to his carrying-on.

Hans Christian was deeply hurt when Edvard refused his suggestion that they be on less formal terms. But he accepted his friend's decision. He wrote to Edvard saying that in their hearts they would always be the closest of friends.

And they were. Edvard helped Hans Christian in many ways. He read through his manuscripts before they were published. He corrected errors and made clean copies. And he took care of his friend's financial matters, which Hans Christian had never learned to handle himself.

Edvard became his lifelong adviser. It was with the Collin family that Hans Christian found his true home, and he visited them almost every day. After his disappointment with Riborg, he needed love and understanding, which he received from Louise Collin.

Louise was just a child when Hans Christian started going to the family home. But now she was a sweet, kind young woman. She had never teased him the way the other children did, and it was her gentle nature that eventually made him stop thinking about Riborg.

Hans Christian's elderly mother still lived in Odense. She was drinking more and more brandy. In July 1832 Hans Christian visited her in the poorhouse for the last time.

His fame gave him no joy, and he felt very ill at ease during this trip. Although he wrote nothing about his mother to his friends, he complained that he wasn't well and was feeling discouraged. But they were used to hearing his complaints, so they paid little attention.

He continued to send money to his mother, but she spent much of it on liquor instead of food or clothes.

One day the governor of Fyn, Prince Christian, insisted on visiting Hans Christian's mother in the poorhouse. It was a great event for Anne Marie.

"Your son has brought you much honor," said the prince, which made her very happy. All the other residents of the poorhouse heard his words, too.

Hans Christian became more and more enchanted with Louise Collin, and he wrote her long, loving letters. She was frightened by his feelings and wrote to him that she was showing his letters to her sister.

Hans Christian was not surprised. That's the way things were back then. He continued to write to her. Now Louise merely had to read between the lines to see how much she meant to him.

But even so, Louise didn't fall in love with Hans Christian. In 1833 she became engaged to a young government official.

Old Jonas Collin, whom Hans Christian often called Father Collin, raised some money so he could travel abroad again.

He headed for Germany, where he already had many friends, and then went as far south as Italy. His travels lasted a year and a half.

He made many friends among the artists in Rome. They praised his sketches and said that he should keep drawing.

Hans Christian's letters and diaries were full of drawings. "How else can I describe everything that I see for all my dear friends back home?" he wrote in one letter.

At the same time he wrote that he had never learned to draw and was lacking in practice. But he probably wanted to encourage praise for his work. "I need praise in order to thrive," he wrote in another letter.

One day Hans Christian received a letter from Denmark that made him very sad. His mother had died.

"Now I'm all alone in the world," he wrote to old Jonas Collin. And he wrote to Henriette Wulff that he felt terrible he hadn't been able to do more for his mother.

In the following years Hans Christian journeyed to both Sweden and Germany. He became one of the best-traveled Danes of his day. This was rather odd, because he was an anxious traveler.

He was afraid of falling ill, and he often suffered from horrible toothaches. He was also afraid of going to sleep for fear that people would think he was dead! When he went to bed at night, he wore a little sign around his neck that read, "I only appear to be dead." He had heard plenty of stories about people who were put in their coffins before they had actually died.

He was afraid of heights, but he would climb the highest mountains. And he usually took rooms on the top floor of a hotel so he could enjoy the view.

He was also afraid of boats, but that didn't stop him from traveling by sea. He would even go out in a small boat to have a view of a city or harbor from the water. He was always conquering his fears, because his curiosity and sense of adventure were greater.

In 1845 the king awarded Hans Christian an annual allowance of six hundred *rigsdaler*. Now he could write more books about his travels. He continued to sketch and write letters, too.

Throughout this time the Collin home in Copenhagen was his haven. It was here and with the Wulff family that he felt a peace and friendship that he could find nowhere else.

In Germany Hans Christian Andersen had become quite famous. He was invited to palaces and manor houses, and other writers wanted to meet him.

When he took his first train trip, he was very nervous.

But he calmed down once the train started moving. He felt like he was being pulled through the landscape by a gentle child. It felt like flying! He saw fields and farms race past. He barely managed to read a few pages in his book before the train reached the next station.

Many people claimed that the pleasures of the traveling life were ruined by rushing along in such a fashion. But Hans Christian disagreed. He knew what it felt like to jolt along poor roads in a coach crowded with passengers. He enjoyed sitting in a comfortable compartment.

"To travel is to live," he said.

And he was always traveling. His longest journey took him to Greece and Turkey. He went as far as Spain, Portugal and North Africa. And he made several trips to Holland, France and England.

He always took two big suitcases and one smaller one with him. They were made of sturdy leather and contained all his belongings. He also took along a hatbox for his top hat, an umbrella, a pair of boots and a walking stick.

In one of the bags he packed a thick rope, which he planned to climb down if fire ever broke out where he was staying. It wasn't easy to flee a burning building in those days. All the stairs were made of wood, and the only place to get water was from the pump in the square.

But neither the difficult journeys nor his dread of illness or fire frightened him so much that he stopped traveling. He enjoyed going to foreign countries and visiting distinguished people.

Hans Christian was getting closer to achieving his goal. But the fact that he would do so by writing fairy tales was something that he didn't realize when he first wrote "several stories for children" back in 1835.

His plays never had the great success that he dreamed of, and the critics continued to judge his novels and poems harshly. He felt far more welcome in Germany than in Denmark, and that made him bitter.

But then the fairy tales were published. Hans Christian described them as "a few trivial pieces." At first no one paid much attention to the book containing four tales: "The Tinderbox," "Little Claus and Big Claus," "The Princess on the Pea" and "Little Ida's Flowers." Then suddenly friends, who were writers, began sending him letters praising them.

Hans Christian didn't know what to think. He had always told stories to the children and grandchildren of his friends. This was nothing new.

Games of all kinds were a constant source of entertainment in the homes that he visited. Guests at the manor houses would often spend the evening telling riddles or composing verses for each other.

There were many different ways that he entertained the children in the households where he stayed. He made intricate paper cutouts, he performed plays, and he gathered bouquets of flowers. He also made shadow puppets with figures that he would hold up in front of a lamp behind a cloth. And he would tell stories with them.

He never dreamed that these little tales were anything special. He was much more preoccupied with his plays and novels than with the stories he wrote in between his more serious pieces.

Throughout the wanderings of his life he still longed for love. Would he ever find love again? he frequently asked himself.

Now he was thirty-eight years old. He often joked that he was already an old bachelor who wrote and traveled, and he was content with that.

CHAPTER NINE

In which we hear about falling in love and becoming famous — and about a sorrow that almost drove Hans Christian mad

In the following years the tales of Hans Christian Andersen became more and more famous. His work was especially loved in Germany.

"You are one of Germany's favorite authors," a noted poet wrote to him.

Hans Christian wrote best when people praised his work, but no one seemed to understand that in Denmark. He was still encountering setbacks there.

Even so, the poor little boy from Odense was a frequent guest of royalty, not only in Denmark and Germany — but all over Europe. His life had become a fairy tale.

As a child he had been given the precious gift of his father telling him stories and reading aloud to him. And the patients at the hospital had also filled his head with sagas and fantasies.

All these stories were hidden inside him and became linked with his own experiences. And then he transformed them into tales.

The story entitled "She Was

96

No Good" is about a washerwoman who drinks. In "The Snow Queen," Hans Christian describes a garden between the eaves of two houses. "The Ugly Duckling" is the story of a swan that goes through terrible times before becoming beautiful and accepted.

He saw a tale in everything he experienced. He even turned his last meeting with Riborg Voigt into a story.

When he met Riborg and her husband, he discovered that he no longer yearned for her. She had been the great love of his youth, but that was over now.

And so he wrote a tale called "The Sweethearts," about a top and a ball. They fail to become sweethearts because the ball is made of fine leather, which makes her too elegant for the simple top.

Hans Christian no longer yearned for Riborg, but he did yearn for love.

Then he met the Swedish singer Jenny Lind, who was singing in the opera in Copenhagen. She had an exceedingly beautiful voice. She was intelligent. And she was fond of both music and art.

He fell in love once again.

Miss Lind was in town for three weeks, and every single day he sent her letters, poems and flowers. He was giddy with infatuation. He thought that he had found true love at last.

Just before Jenny Lind returned to Sweden, Hans Christian handed her a letter and begged her to understand the feelings expressed in it.

She understood, and although she was fond of him and admired him, she did not love him.

Hans Christian wrote to her and asked her to marry him, but she turned him down. They saw each other again two years later, and she treated him like a brother — not like a sweetheart.

He proposed again the following year, but she replied that there could be no question of marriage for the two of them.

They met again in Berlin, spending New Year's Eve together. Jenny had her female chaperone with her. It was a beautiful and poetic evening. Jenny sang for Hans Christian in a parlor decorated with pine boughs and Christmas stars. And then an article about them appeared in the newspaper. It was a story about two artists who both came from poor circumstances and who had spent New Year's Eve together in splendid surroundings.

That was the end of their love.

Jenny Lind married someone else, and Hans Christian once again faced his loneliness. But the whole affair became a story called "The Nightingale." This is one of his best-known and most loved tales. It is the story of a little gray forest bird that is not admired as much as a mechanical bird encrusted with diamonds and other gems.

Hans Christian Andersen was now a famous man. By the mid to late 1840s his tales had been translated into English and were published in America. He was well known all over Europe. And finally people in Denmark also loved his stories. He was awarded his first medal, the German Order of the Scarlet Eagle. He attended dinner parties wearing elegant attire, and was friends with dukes and kings.

He wrote to his friends about his triumphs and about all the gifts and invitations he received. But he still wasn't happy.

Most of all, he wished for recognition from old Jonas Collin. If Father Collin didn't regard him as a genius, then all the honors showered on him meant very little. Yet both Jonas and Edvard Collin remained silent. They were fond of Hans Christian for his own sake — not because he was famous. They weren't the sort to

offer lavish words of praise. They loved him in their own way.

He had proof of this when old Mrs. Collin died. He was the only person outside the family who was summoned to her deathbed.

The Collin household was still an important part of Hans Christian's life. He was very fond of the children, and he enjoyed sewing and making paper cutouts with them. He also made Christmas decorations, and he never forgot their birthdays.

He often took several of the older children along with him when he traveled. It certainly wouldn't do them any harm to see how well he was received at court all over Europe! And it wouldn't hurt if they happened to talk about this at home in Copenhagen.

It was during this period that he started to write about his life. The result was his famous autobiography, *The Fairy Tale of My Life*. In this memoir he describes growing up poor in Odense and his life as a youth in both Copenhagen and Slagelse. He also writes about his life as a poet and about his books and plays.

The book was a great achievement. It was published in Denmark in 1855, when Hans Christian Andersen was fifty years old. Letters poured in from people who admired both him and his art.

He had triumphed. He had attained his life's goal. But he also had to endure great sorrows.

In 1858 fire broke out on board the steamship *Austria* in the middle of the Atlantic. One of the passengers was his beloved friend Henriette Wulff. And she was not among the survivors.

When he heard the news Hans Christian wept in great despair. He reproached himself for not writing to Henriette more often. He pictured her throwing herself into the sea, surrounded by flames. His imagination would give him no peace, and he nearly went mad. It took all his strength to cope with his grief. He eventually recovered, although all his life his fragile sense of balance was easily disturbed.

Edvard Collin's wife was one of the people who lovingly tended to him when he was grieving for Henriette. She listened to his cries and laments. She comforted him and encouraged him. But every once in a while even she would exclaim, "Oh, now he's going too far!"

Her little daughter shared this feeling. Whenever she came home and saw Hans Christian's big galoshes in the foyer, she would say, "Is that awful Mr. Andersen here again?"

Then her mother would scold her and say, "Just remember that it was Mr. Andersen who wrote 'The Nightingale.'"

Little Louise loved that story, but she did not love Mr. Andersen.

Yet most children did. They didn't see him as Louise did, pacing the parlor and waving his big handkerchief as he wept and whined. Nor did they see how he was calmed and soothed, and then shortly afterwards sat down to eat a whole platter of sandwiches.

Most children thought of him as a kindly old uncle. And he was like an uncle in the home of Edvard Collin. But the entire family

continued to treat him as they always had, before he was famous. And Hans Christian found that difficult to understand.

He made new friends with the Henriques and Melchior families. He felt especially comfortable in the Melchior household, where art and music and literature were everyday topics of conversation. Theirs was a warm and lively family, and they understood his sensitive nature and delicate nerves. They were considerate of him and his eccentricities, and he often stayed at their home.

CHAPTER TEN

In which we hear about the writer
who became an honorary
citizen of his birthplace

Hans Christian Andersen's numerous and lengthy travels gave him ample material for new tales. He wrote about mountains and rushing rivers, about the storks on the Nile and about migratory birds that spent the winter in Africa. He studied the flight of various birds and read about their habits. Many of his tales feature animals and flowers.

Hans Christian had a very special feeling for flowers. He had scores of potted plants in his apartment in the Nyhavn district of Copenhagen. When he visited friends he would often take a bouquet of his own flowers to the hostess. His bouquets were nothing like the fancy arrangements that other guests purchased. They were often quite simple — a single flowering sprig, a couple of lilies and some greenery. He also made flower wreaths that he would give away, and he was often asked to provide centerpieces when his friends planned lavish dinner parties.

In his apartment there was a room that was unheated, and he would put the dormant plants in this "winter room" during the dark season. When the sun and heat returned, he would take the plants back into the parlor, and they would bloom.

Yet even in the winter he would make bouquets as gifts. He might find some evergreen branches in the woods, or a lovely withered rose. Then he would put them together with an artist's touch. No one was ever able to copy him.

He brought home both plant cuttings and seeds from his trips. These he also planted and tended carefully.

In his diary Hans Christian writes about melons from Africa. He managed to get the plants to flower, but the fruit fell off. He also had African cactuses in his parlor. Every evening he would move them away from the chill of the windows because they couldn't tolerate the cold.

When he was traveling, he often sent letters to his friends containing a little floral greeting — tiny dried flowers taped to a card. He also enjoyed dried flowers as a reminder of his experiences. And he put floral designs in the intricate paper cutouts that he made for both children and adults.

Finally Hans Christian was about to have the greatest triumph of his life. He had been named an honorary citizen of Odense.

The event was celebrated on December 6, 1867. The temperature was icy when he arrived in the town of his birth. He was shivering and nursing a cold. And, as so often before, he was suffering from a terrible toothache.

Hans Christian was very nervous. He grew even more nervous when he heard that the schoolchildren were to be given a free day, and that the whole town was going to be decorated in his honor.

Everyone had read his account of the fortune-teller in his autobiography. Now it was time to make her prediction come true. All of Odense would be lit up. The great writer would be hailed by one and all, in gratitude for the tales he had given them.

He stood on the steps of the town hall and listened to the cheers rising toward him.

What a triumph! Here he had lived as a poor boy. Here his lunatic grandfather had been teased by the street urchins. Here his father and mother had struggled to earn enough to feed him. And now here he was, an honorary citizen of the town!

His toothache was almost unbearable, and his nerves were making him shake. What would everyone in Copenhagen say about such an homage? Would they think him ridiculous and once again mock him, calling him vain?

But he need not have feared. The big newspapers in Copenhagen all wrote about his triumph, saying that he certainly deserved the great honor.

Afterwards there was a festive dinner at the town hall. Telegrams poured in, and there was even one from the king. Hans Christian enjoyed the praise and speeches and songs. But his toothache got worse and worse. After dinner he stood at an open window, looking down at the Town Hall Square. The ice cold wind made his tooth throb.

A song had been specially written for the occasion, and he sighed

when he saw how many verses there were. How was he going to
stay on his feet until the end? Thousands of torches and smiling faces
lit up the square. When the song was over, everyone threw their
torches onto a great bonfire. That was the grand finale.

Hundreds of people wanted to shake hands with him. He was
both happy and proud. He had made it through the festivities. The
day was over — and his toothache vanished in a matter of minutes.

Now he could finally go to bed.

But he couldn't sleep. Too many thoughts were swirling through
his mind after the long, eventful day.

CHAPTER ELEVEN

In which we hear about the old writer,
his friends — and his last days

Hans Christian Andersen was now an old man. He was often ill, but he seldom stayed in bed. He went to the theater almost every evening when he was in Copenhagen. And he continued to write fairy tales. He also still made beautiful paper cutouts for his friends and their children. He was no longer afraid of being criticized. He was so famous he had nothing to fear.

Yet he remained a very nervous person, and his imagination made him extraordinarily sensitive. He would jump at loud noises, and he had terrible nightmares.

In his own peculiar way, he was a handsome man. Every day he would have the barber curl his hair, and he was still very particular about his clothes. When he entered a room on special occasions, everyone would turn to look at him. His black attire and white scarf suited him. Around his neck he would wear a medal on a blue ribbon. And he still had the ability to make people listen to him.

But he was in poor health. He coughed and suffered from stomach ailments. The winter of 1874 was particularly hard.

When summer came, he went to visit the Melchior family at Tranquility, their country estate on the coast of Øresund. He lay in bed, dictating letters to Mrs. Melchior, who nursed him.

Ten days before he died, Hans Christian received a letter from Edvard Collin's son asking him to join him on his travels abroad. He dictated a reply at once. He said that he would very much like to go along, but at the moment he was sick in bed. He ended the letter with "See you soon!"

Mrs. Melchior added a postscript. She wrote that he was gravely ill, and his strength was declining with each day. But he was in good spirits and possessed infinite patience.

"Apart from this cough, the weariness, and my swollen feet, I'm in perfect health," he told Mrs. Melchior, as she sat by his bedside. He would doze off, but whenever he woke, he would smile at her.

On August 4, 1875, at eleven in the morning, Hans Christian Andersen died, calmly and peacefully.

A fairy tale life was over.

Groundwood Books / House of Anansi Press
110 Spadina Avenue, Suite 801, Toronto, Ontario M5V 2K4
Distributed in the USA by Publishers Group West
1700 Fourth Street, Berkeley, CA 94710

Library and Archives Canada Cataloging in Publication
Varmer, Hjørdis
Hans Christian Andersen : His Fairy Tale Life / by Hjørdis Varmer ;
illustrated by Lilian Brøgger ;
translated by Tiina Nunnally.
Translation of: Den fattige dreng fra Odense.
ISBN 0-88899-690-X
1. Andersen, H.C. (Hans Christian), 1805-1875–Juvenile literature. 2. Authors,
Danish–19th century–Biography–Juvenile literature. I. Brøgger, Lilian II.
Nunnally, Tiina III. Title.
PT8119.V3713 2005   j839.81'36   C2005-900567-X

Printed and bound in China

Further Reading

For young readers:

The Amazing Paper Cuttings of Hans Christian Andersen by Beth Wagner Brust. Boston: Houghton Mifflin, 2003.

Fairy Tales by Hans Christian Andersen, translated by Tiina Nunnally, edited and introduced by Jackie Wullschlager. New York: Viking, 2005.

A Perfect Wizard: Hans Christian Andersen by Jane Yolen, illustrated by Dennis Nolan. New York: Dutton Children's Books, 2004.

The Stories of Hans Christian Andersen: A New Translation from the Danish by Jeffrey Frank and Diana Crone Frank. Boston: Houghton Mifflin, 2003.

For older readers:

The Fairy Tale of My Life by Hans Christian Andersen. New York: Cooper Square Press, 2000.

Hans Christian Andersen by Jens Andersen, translated by Tiina Nunnally. New York: The Overlook Press, 2005.

Hans Christian Andersen: The Life of a Storyteller by Jackie Wullschlager. New York: Penguin, 2005.